First American edition 1989.
First published by William Heinemann Ltd.
Printed in the Netherlands
First impression
Library of Congress Cataloging-in-Publication Data
Cole. Babette. Three cheers for Errol! / Babette Cole. — 1st
American ed. p. cm.
Summary: Errol the city rat uses his brain
as well as his athletic ability when he competes in the Inter-school
Ratathalon. [1. Rats—Fiction. 2. Sports—Fiction.]
I. Title. PZ7.C6734Th 1989 [E]—dc19 88-27618 CIP AC
ISBN 0-399-21671-5

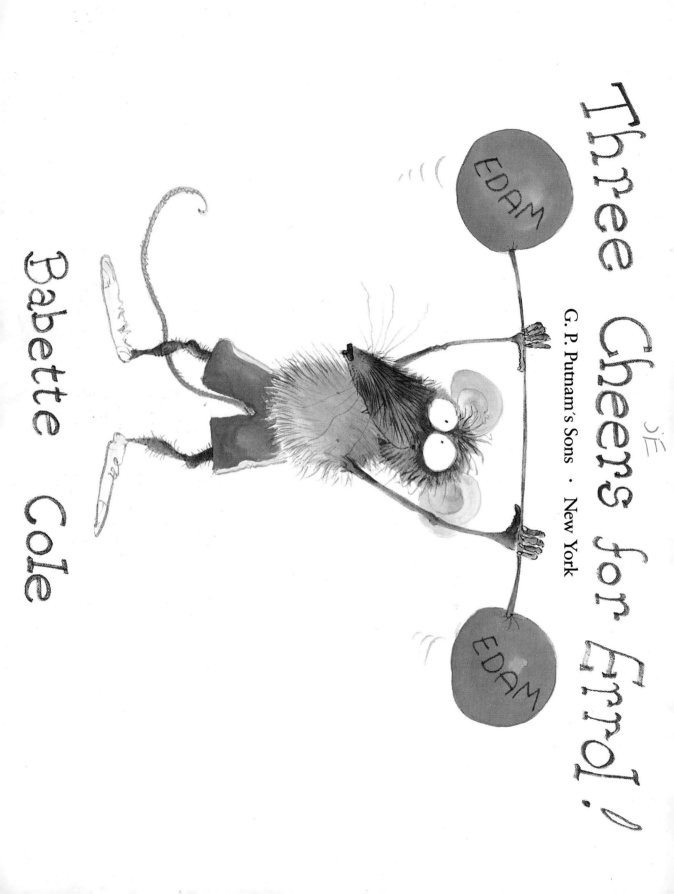

Three Cheers for Errol!

Babette Cole

G. P. Putnam's Sons · New York

Errol was a city rat.
He went to a scruffy school in a drain.

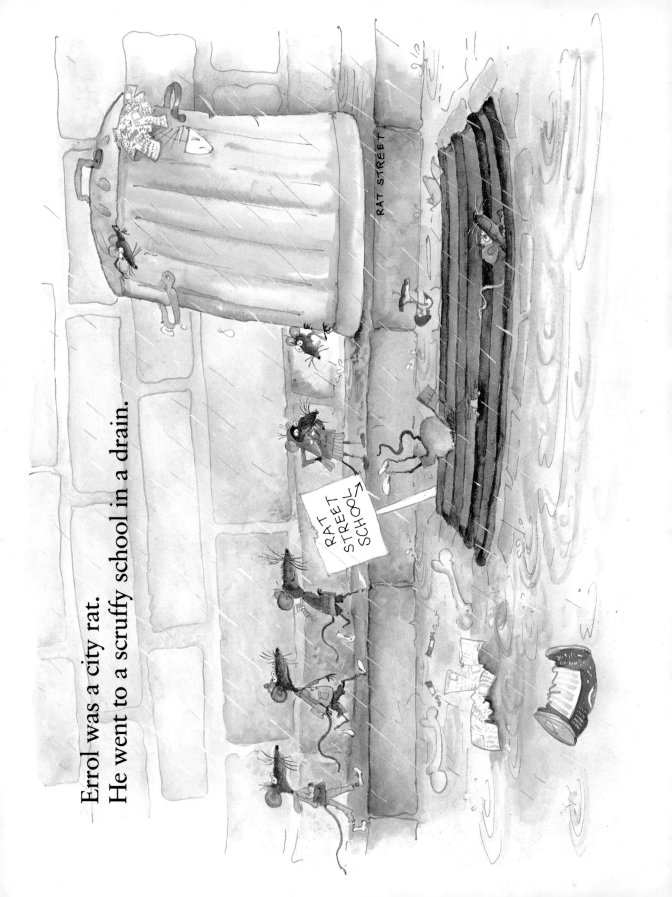

He was bad at math.

He was bad at spelling.

POOI!

He was bad at science.

He was bad at art.
"You're dumb, Errol!" everyone said.

But every day, after school, Errol rushed home to practice something he was really good at . . .

. . . SPORTS!

In fact, he was so good at sports that he was chosen to represent his school in the Inter-school Ratathalon, even though everyone thought he was dumb.

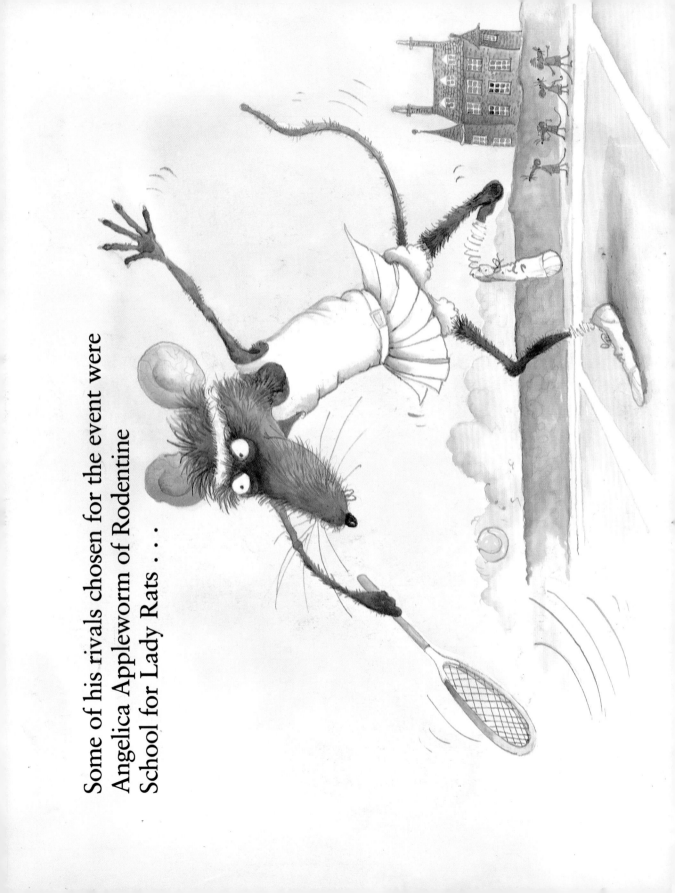

Some of his rivals chosen for the event were
Angelica Appleworm of Rodentine
School for Lady Rats . . . .

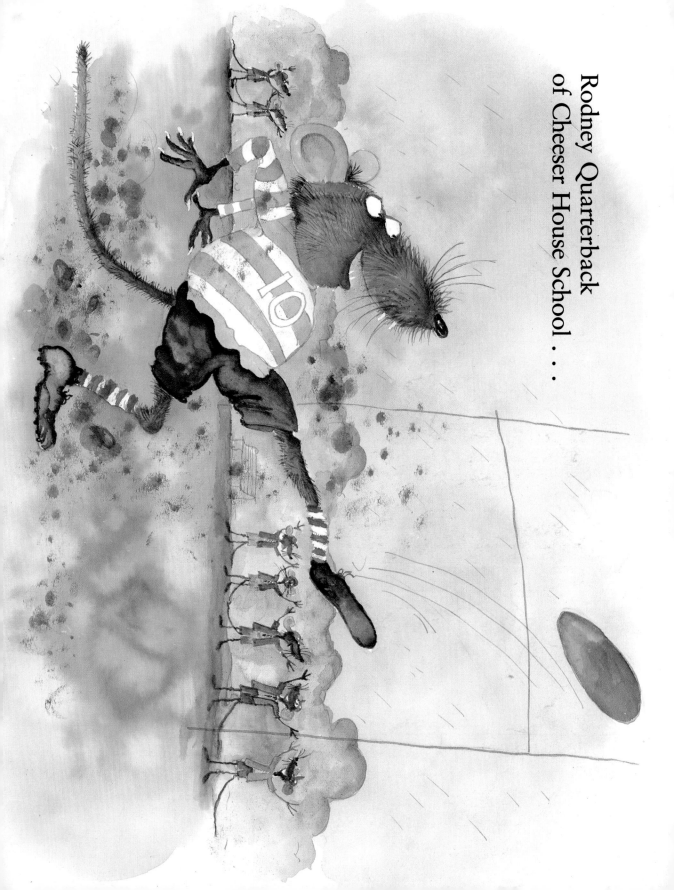

Rodney Quarterback
of Cheeser House School . . .

. . . and Jasintha O'Wiska from
St. Rattingund's Convent.

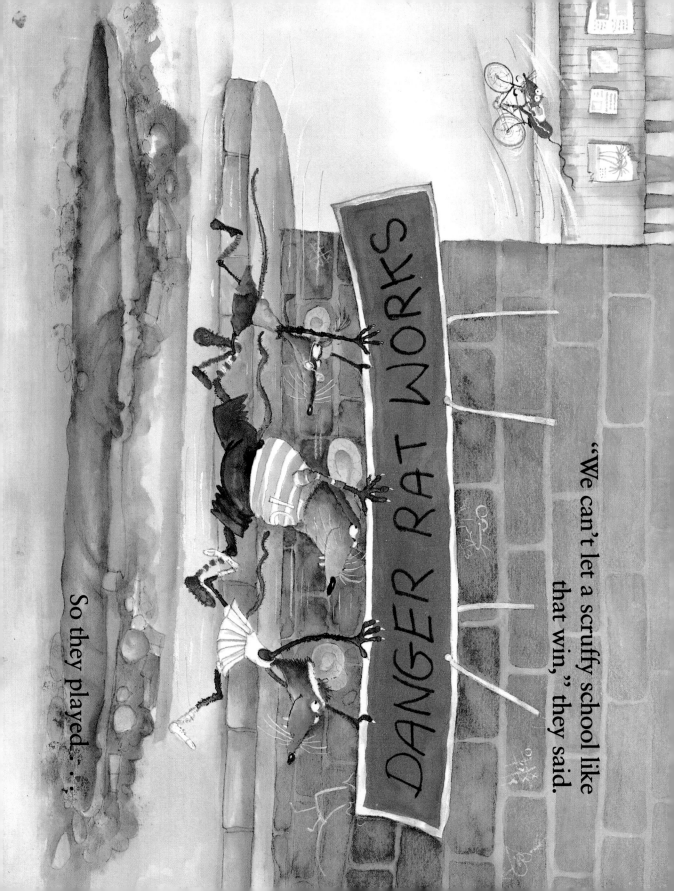

DANGER RAT WORKS

"We can't let a scruffy school like that win," they said.

So they played....

. . . a dirty trick on Errol!

Errol was in a bad way.

"I wish I had an extra leg," said Errol.

"I could do that," he said.

Outside he saw some street acrorats. Errol had a brainstorm!

So he went back into training.

When Errol arrived at the Ratathalon, all the other competitors laughed.

But he won the twenty-five meter sprint!

And the high jump!

WHEEEEE

And the javelin throw!

And the swimming race!

"What a smart rat!" they said.

Three cheers for Errol!